All Kinds of Children

Norma Simon

ILLUSTRATED BY Diane Paterson

ALBERT WHITMAN & COMPANY * MORTON GROVE, ILLINOIS

For Debbie and Jon, with love. —N. S.

For John and Peter Pan, who keep
the child inside young and wise. —D. P.

Also by Norma Simon

All Kinds of Families * Cats Do, Dogs Don't * How Do I Feel?

I Am Not a Crybaby * I'm Busy, Too * I Was So Mad! * I Wish I Had My Father

Mama Cat's Year * Nobody's Perfect, Not Even My Mother * Oh, That Cat!

The Saddest Time * What Do I Do? * Why Am I Different?

Library of Congress Cataloging-in-Publication Data
Simon, Norma.
All kinds of children / by Norma Simon; illustrated by Diane Paterson.
p. cm.
Summary: Presents the things that children all over the world have in common, including their need for food,
clothes, people to love them, and the opportunity to play.
ISBN 0-8075-0281-2
1. Children—Pictorial works—Juvenile literature. 2. Children—Juvenile literature. [1. Children.]
I. Paterson, Diane, 1956- ill. II. Title. HQ781.5.S56 1999 305.23'022'2—dc21 98-36356 CIP AC

The illustrations were done with watercolors and pencils.
The text is set in Artcraft.
The design is by Scott Piehl.

Young children love to compare themselves to others. "Just like me!" is the happy response as a child recognizes that another boy or girl loves to eat apples or has a new baby in the family. Making comparisons helps a child gradually build the "me" of his or her individual personality.

As children compare themselves to others, they are also looking to be reassured that they are just like other kids. This book will help children realize all they have in common with other boys and girls, not only in their community but around the world. It will help them become aware that while there are many fascinating differences, at the core all children are the same. All need food and clothes; all like to run and play; all want to love and be loved.

By showing your children that they are part of the larger world, you can help them grow up to be caring, responsible citizens. For while we can learn about and celebrate the many differences between cultures and countries, our awareness and appreciation of the important ways we are alike will help us live together in peace.

Norma Simon

Do you know
that every child in the whole world
has a bellybutton?
Just like YOU!
All over the world,
children are the same.

All children need food—
milk, cereal, meat,
vegetables and juicy fruit,
rice and pasta and bread—
food to help them grow
big and strong and smart,
just like you.

All children need clothes—
diapers and shirts,
pants and dresses,
hats and coats,
all kinds of shoes!

All over the world,
children live in houses.
Some houses are big,
some are small.
Some are way up high,
some are on the water.
Some children stay in the
same house for a long time.
Some children move from place to place.

All children need people to love them—
mommies and daddies,
sisters and brothers,

grandmas and grandpas,

aunts and uncles, stepparents and foster parents,
caregivers and teachers, neighbors and friends.

All children like to hold something special—
blankets or pacifiers,
teddy bears or dolls.
They like to hold them close,
especially when they feel tired or sad.

All children like to play.
They dig in the dirt,
they splash in water.
They build roads and bridges
for their cars and trucks.
They play games
like hide-and-go-seek.
Children love to just *run*.
What do you like to play?

Children do work, too.
They clean the house.
They help with cooking.
They help with babies.
They help their families.
What work do you do?

Children all over the world
love to go for rides—
on a bus, in a wagon,
on a boat, train, or plane,
on a donkey or pony,
or snuggled in a pack!

All children love stories.
They like to sit on soft laps
and listen ...
to old stories, new stories,
long stories, short stories,
real stories, and pretend stories.
What is your favorite story?

All children go to sleep at night.
They climb into all kinds of beds;
they dream different dreams.

Do you know
that every grownup in the whole world
used to be a baby?
Mommies, daddies,
grandmas, grandpas,
firefighters, truck drivers, teachers, too—
they all were babies once,
just like you used to be.

All over the world,
children are growing.
Little by little,
year by year,
children grow and grow.
And one day, someday soon,
they will be all grown up.
And so will YOU!